RICHARD SCARRY'S
Great Big Schoolhouse
Readers

A Smelly Story

Illustrated by Huck Scarry
Written by Erica Farber

STERLING

New York / London
www.sterlingpublishing.com/kids

Huckle put on his watch.

"What time is it?" asked Lowly.

"Time to take out the garbage," said Mrs. Cat.

Huckle's watch went BEEP! BEEP!

The bag was big.

The bag was heavy.

Oops!

The garbage fell.

Huckle fell.

His watch fell into
the garbage.

"What time is it?"
asked Lowly.
"Time for breakfast,"
said Mrs. Cat.

Huckle looked down. Oh, no!
His watch was gone.

The garbage was gone, too.

"There goes your watch,"
said Lowly.

"Let's go!" said Huckle.

"After that truck!"

Bridget came, too.

9

They rode fast.

They rode faster.

But the truck went the fastest!

The truck stopped at the dock.

The truck dumped the garbage.

Whoosh!

Now the garbage was on a boat.

The boat started to go.

Arthur was in a small boat.

He was fishing with his dad.

14

Huckle, Bridget, and
Lowly got into the boat.
"Go!" said Huckle.
"After that boat, please."

The boat went up the river.

It went to a place full of garbage.

The place was very smelly.

Huckle waved to the driver.
"My watch is in the garbage!"
he called.

Huckle hopped on the boat.

His friends did, too.

They looked and looked
for Huckle's watch.

All they found
was smelly garbage.

BEEP! BEEP!

They all jumped.

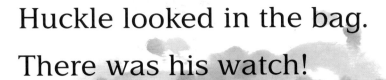

Huckle looked in the bag.
There was his watch!

"What time is it?" asked Lowly.

"Time to take a bath," said Huckle.

STERLING and the distinctive Sterling logo are registered trademarks of Sterling Publishing Co., Inc.

Library of Congress Cataloging-in-Publication Data Available

Lot #: 10 9 8 7 6 5 4 3 2 1
03/11
Published by Sterling Publishing Co., Inc.
387 Park Avenue South, New York, NY 10016

In association with JB Publishing, Inc.
121 West 27th Street, Suite 902, New York, NY 10001

Distributed in Canada by Sterling Publishing
c/o Canadian Manda Group, 165 Dufferin Street
Toronto, Ontario, Canada M6K 3H6
Distributed in the United Kingdom by GMC Distribution Services
Castle Place, 166 High Street, Lewes, East Sussex, England BN7 1XU
Distributed in Australia by Capricorn Link (Australia) Pty. Ltd.
P.O. Box 704, Windsor, NSW 2756, Australia

produced by ●JR Sansevere

4650 1713 8/11

Sterling ISBN: 978-1-4027-8445-3 (hardcover)
               978-1-4027-7319-8 (paperback)

For information about custom editions, special sales, premium and corporate purchases, please contact Sterling Special Sales Department at 800-805-5489 or specialsales@sterlingpublishing.com.